MW01624319

DOG MAN AND CAT KID

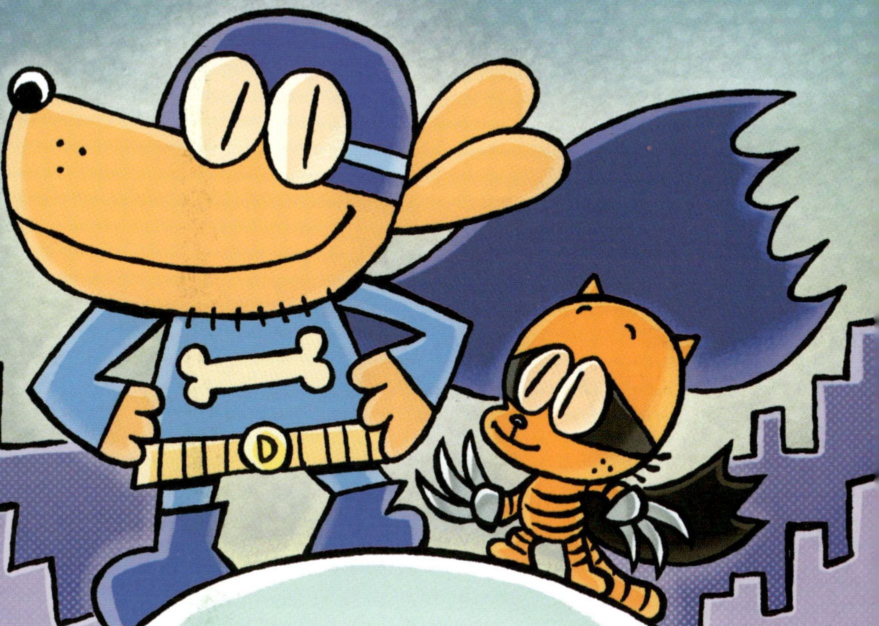

WRITTEN AND ILLUSTRATED BY DAV PILKEY
AS GEORGE BEARD AND HAROLD HUTCHINS
WITH COLOR BY JOSE GARIBALDI

AN IMPRINT OF
SCHOLASTIC

FOR A REAL HERO, BILLY DIMICHELE

With thanks to John Steinbeck, whose novels, particularly East of Eden, still resonate with readers today.

Library of Congress Control Number 2017939754

978-93-5275-545-5

Printed in India
First edition, January 2018
This edition April 2022

Edited by Anamika Bhatnagar
Book design by Dav Pilkey and Phil Falco
Color by Jose Garibaldi
Creative Director: David Saylor

CHAPTERS

DOG MAN

Behind the Scenes

What up, Poochies? We're George and Harold!

Me too!

That means we're totally mature!

And deep, too, y'all!

AnyHoo, our new teacher has been making us read all of these old-timey books lately.

East of Eden

Those aren't monocles! They're just rings from plastic milk jugs!
What? We can't use our imaginations anymore?

So we started making a brand-new Dog Man graphic novel!

But before we begin, Let's recap our story thus Far...

One time, a cop and a police dog...

...got hurt in an explosion!
KA BLOOEY

In the hospital, the doctor gave them sad news.
BOO HOO!

Your head is dying, cop.
aw, man!

And your body is dying, dog!
whine whine

But then, the nurse lady got a great idea!

Let's sew the dog's head onto cop's body!!!
You're a Genius!!!
Hooray!

So they had a big operation.

And Like a warrior born of adversity...

...a hero arose from the ashes!
HOORAY FOR DOG MAN!

Along the way, Dog Man has made some great friends...
Sarah Hatoff: World's greatest reporter
chief
Chief: World's greatest Chief
ZUZU: World's greatest Poodle

...And one terrible enemy.
I'LL GET YOU, DOG MAN--- IF it's The LAST Thing I DO!
Petey: World's evilest cat

In our Last story, Petey tried to make a clone of himself.
U
CLone 'em

But his clone was a kitten.
DNA Chute
StarT

Things went from bad...

... to worse.
Free KiTTY

But one Lucky night, all of that changed.
Free KiTTY

Li'L Petey found a new home...
DOG man
Free Kitty

...but can he escape his destiny?

Tree-House Comix Proudly Presents
Chapter 1
The Kitty Sitter
by George and Harold

Early one morning...
DOG Man

CLANK
CLANK
DOG Man

DOG Man
CLANK

CLANK
CLANK

CLANK
CLANK

KA-KLIK
RATCH RATCH RATCH
RATCH RATCH RATCH
Z Z Z Z
SLEEPY KITTY
RATCH
RATCH RATCH RATCH

Good morning, Dog Man!

I'm fixing my Robot, 80-HD!

Ring
Ring

Ring
Ring
Ring

DOG MAN!

It's Me, Chief!
You're LATE Again!
chief

GET TO WORK NOW!

YOO-HOO!

HeLLo, there!!!

Please allow me to introduce myself.
Dog Man

I'm Mrs. Suspicionflame, the world's greatest baby-sitter!!!

Here's my card...

...and my impressive List of references.

munch
munch
munch

I specialize in cat-sitting...
Dog Man

...and I can start Today!

SLURP

Kiss
Kiss
Kiss
Kiss

Bye, Dog Man! Have fun at work!

Well, uh--- hello there, young man.
Hi, Papa.

I AM NOT YOUR PAPA!
Dog Man
Yes you are!

I'm a professional governess! I've got a British accent and everything!

I sing songs about how much fun it is to clean up your room and stuff!
OK, Prove it!
Sing me a song.

OK, I WILL!

Hmmm...

Just a spoonful of high-fructose corn syrup...

...gives the medicine Possible side-effects which may include...

...nausea, headaches, dry mouth, runny nose...

...and Diarrhea!

Uh---Look--
can you hand me the vise grip?

Yeah. Here ya go.
Thanks.

What'cha doing?
I'm fixing 80-HD!

Hey! Did you add solar panels?
Yeah.

Wow! You can't even see 'em!

INteresting!!!
Thanks!

HeY! Where Are All the Missiles?
I took 'em out!

WHY?
80-HD is my friend. He doesn't need missiles!

80-HD is NOT Your Friend!
Yes he is!
Here---I'll show ya!
Flip yourself over, 80-HD!
See?

He's Just OBEYING You!

I Programmed him to do that!!!

Obedience does NOT equal friend-ship!!!

He's still my friend!
No He's NOT!

First You remove his missiles...

Then you give him SOLAR PANELS!

How does he get any power at night?
He doesn't.

He sleeps at night just like me!

THAT DOES IT!

YOU AND I NEED to have a TALK!
No we don't.

YES, WE DO!
No we don't!
YES, WE DO!
No we don't!
YES, WE DO!
No we don't!
YES, WE DO!
No we don't!!!!!
Look---I'll buy you some ice cream!
OK! Let's go!

Chapter 2

HOLLYWOOD HERO

by George and Harold

Meanwhile...
Uh... heh-heh...
COPS
COPS

Dog Man should be here any minute.
Chief

Is he **ALWAYS** this late?
Yeah--- but, well, he's a maverick!
Chief

He plays by his own rules...
Chief

...but he gets the job done!
COPS
COPS

He's the thinking man's Rin tin Tin!!!
chief

He's tough...
He's serious...
chief
SPROING!

NOOOOO!
chief

CUT IT OUT
chief
GET OFF!
QUIT!
STOP!
BAD DOGGY!
WHY?

WHY DO WE HAVE TO GO THROUGH THIS EVERY DAY?
chief

ahem.
chief

Oh yeah. Dog Man, this is Sam Hamilton.

He's a big-time Hollywood Director!
Lick

He's gonna make a movie about you!
chief

That's right. It's the true story of a Hero!
THE DOG-MAN
chief

It's got depth, intelligence, and passion...
Wow! Just Like **our** stories!
chief
Right, Dog Man?

chief
munch
munch
munch
THE DOG-MAN

Hey! Gimme that Poster!
chief
THE DOG-MAN

GiVE it!!!
chief
THE DOG-MAN

Ha-Ha--- He always does this!
chief

R-RiP

chief
THE DOG-MAN

Here ya go!
THE DOG-MAN
chief

chief
CRUSH

No! I can't work with him!
crumple crumple

He is an IDIOT!!!

But he's the best cop we've got!!!
ABC
cookies
chief

OK! I'll give him one more chance!
chief

This is Yolay Caprese!
chief

She's the world's greatest actress!
chief

chief
HEY!

* Italian for "hello." (Pronounced "chow.")

Yeah, but he's a Bum! He eats everything and he's always Late!
chief

** TransLation: Hello, handsome!

I have a job for you!

But---
You shall be my bodyguard!

But--
And I Shall reward you...

But-
...with **Tummy Rubs!**

INTRODUCING
FLIP

STEP 1.
First, place your left hand inside the dotted lines marked "Left hand here." Hold the book open FLAT!

STEP 2:
Grasp the right-hand page with your thumb and index finger (inside the dotted lines marked "Right Thumb Here").

STEP 3:
Now QUICKLY flip the right-hand page back and forth until the picture appears to be Animated.

(For extra fun, try adding your own sound-effects!)

Remember,

while you are flipping, be sure you can see the image on page 43 **AND** the image on page 45.

If you flip quickly, the two pictures will start to look like one **ANIMATED** cartoon!

Don't forget to add your own sound-effects!

Left hand here.

Right Thumb here.

OK! Let's go make a movie!
But- But-
Oh, boy! This is gonna be Great!

Dog Man's gonna be a famous body-guard!

And I bet he won't make ANY mistakes this time!

Ain't that right, DOG Man?

munch munch munch

Chapter 3

The Talk

Ice cream, Here we come!
DOG MAN

Hey! Where do you think **YOU'RE** going?
DOG MAN

He's coming with us!
Sorry, kid!

Make him stay here!
But why?

Just make him stay here--- or **NO ICE CREAM!**

Wait here for me, 80-HD!

Ten Minutes Later

Here ya go, kid!
ICE CREAM
Thank you!

How's the ice cream?
good.

I'm sorry I had to trick you with this disguise.

You didn't trick me!

ALRight, SmarTY-Pants! Go ahead and be **MEAN!!!**

But you don't understand how I **Suffer!**

The cops are lookin' **everywhere** for me!

They're gonna put me back in jail and throw away the key!!!

I've got nowhere to hide...

... and nobody to help me!!!

I'm all alone!!!

I'll help you, Papa!

Do you Promise?
Yeah!

Great! I'm gonna move in with you guys...

... and we can continue your EVIL TRAINING!

But I don't wanna be evil, Papa.

Would You STOP Calling me PAPA? I'm NOT Your PAPA!

You're MY CLONE!

That means you and me are the SAME!

I'm evil, so you have to be evil, too!

You don't have any CHOICE in the matter!

But I wanna be Perfect Like Dog Man!
DOG MAN ISN'T Perfect! He's A GOODY-GOODY MILK-TOAST GUMDROP!!

Yep! I'm an escaped convict, and you promised to help me!

That's called "**HARBORING A FUGITIVE.**"

That's against the law!
It is?

Yep! It's a FELONY!

And Look at this SideWALK!
You dripped ICE CReAM All over it!!!

That's Littering!

You're --- You're a MONSTER!

And now You're
JAYWALKING!

Boy, you really ARE EVIL!

Maybe I should be taking lessons from YOU!
Please don't Litter

Please don't Litter

Please don't Litter

Give your-
self to the
DARK Side!
PLease
don't
Litter

It is Your
DESTINY!

PLease
don't
Litter
PLOP!

My
Son!

Chapter 4

An Aching Kind of Growing

By George and Harold

Hi, I'm Sarah Hatoff, the world's greatest reporter.

Today is the 1st day of shooting for the new DoG Man movie...

... and the crowds are bursting with excitement!!!
STUDIO
Hooray

Let's meet some of the fans!

Oh, Look! It's Li'L Petey!

Hi, Sarah. Hi, Zuzu!

You must be the nanny! Are you excited about the Dog Man movie?

DOG MAN MOVIE?!!?

That's the DUMBest Movie idea EVER!!!
Sniff Sniff

Grrrrr!
Be nice, Zuzu!

Yeah! Be nice, Zuzu!!!
BARK BARK BARK

Oh, Look! Here come the stars!

Wow! It's international action hero Ding-Dong Magoo!!!

I'll be playing Dog Man!

Dog Man doesn't have muscles!

Next, it's YoLay Caprese. She'll be playing **me**!!!

Viva l'Italia!*
(* Hooray for Italy!)

But I'm Australian!

Here comes Samson J. Johnson as "Chief"!

ENOUGH IS ENOUGH!!!

I have HAD IT with these DOG-GONE ACTORS in this DOG-GONE LIMO!!!

And finally, it's comic Superstar Scooter McRibs!

Hiya, Dummies! I'll be playing Petey the cat!

That guy doesn't look ANYTHING like me--- er, I mean, like PETEY!
Grrrrr

GASSY BEHEMOTH STUDIOS
And now, Let's enter the studio...

... and go behind the scenes!!!

Wow! Look at all this STUFF!!!

These miniature buildings are so REALISTIC!!!

Ooh... and what are these?
EDEN

These are the robotic Hot Dogs for the big action scene in Act 3.
EDEN

And check out our Pièce de résistance!*
EDEN
MECHA-BOTS
* (French for: Supa Awesomest thingy)

It's **PhiLLY The GYRO!**
Nah-he's just another robot we buiLt!
EDEN

I controL 'em all with this compLicated Remote!
EDEN

ON
OFF
Good
Evil

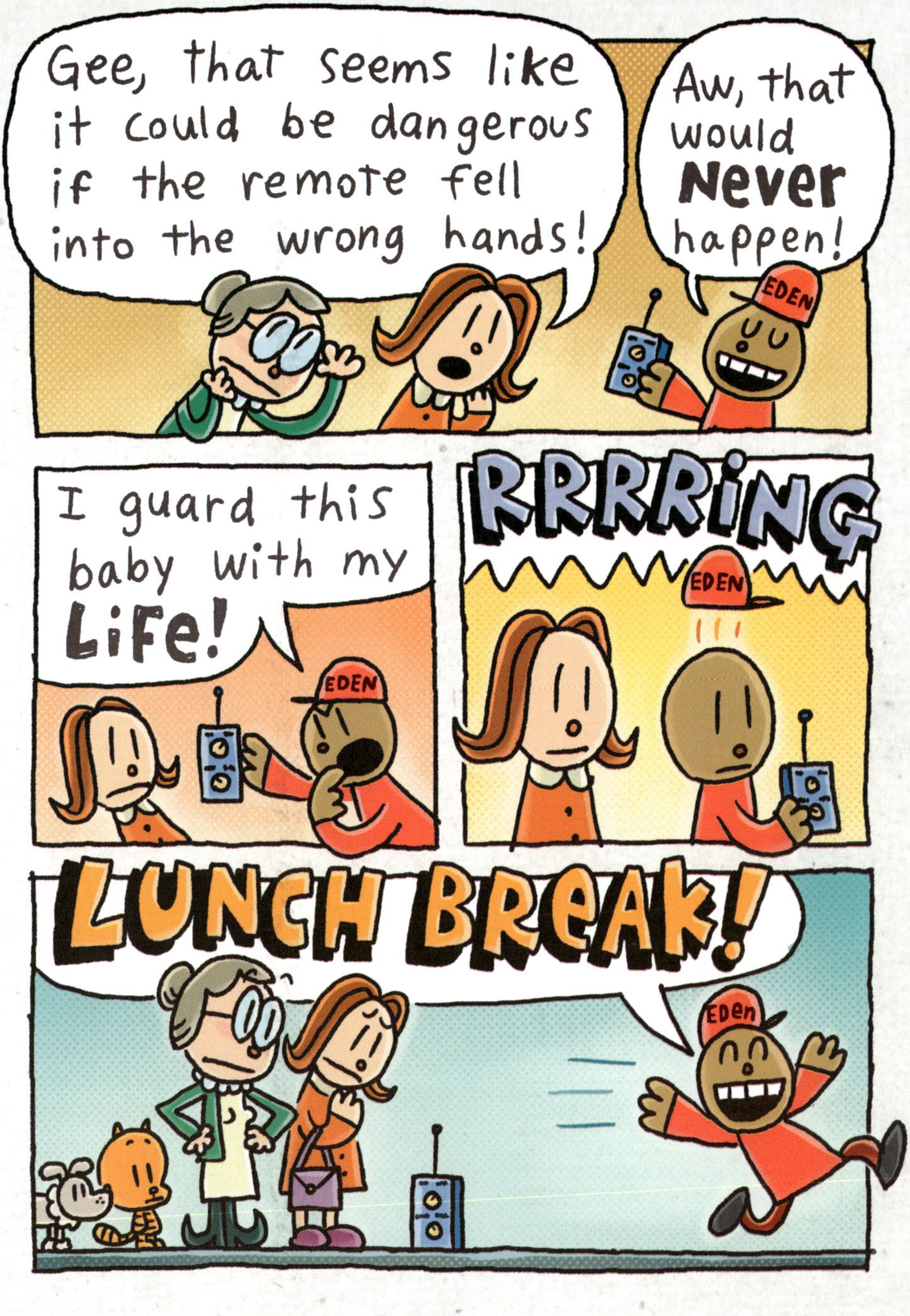

I guard this baby with my **LIFE!**

EDEN

RRRRING

EDEN

LUNCH BREAK!

EDEN

ON OFF
GOOD EVIL

Hey---Look OUT!
ON OFF
GOOD EVIL

Well, C'mon, darling! It's time to go!
Bye-bye!
?

Are we goin' home?
No WAY!

We're gonna have some FUN!!!
costumes

RATS! The door is Locked!
COSTUMES

Hey, go through this pet flap and unlock the door!

Gee, I don't know...
Do it for FUN!

Yeah, but–
Do it for ADVENTURE!

I know, but...
Do it for Papa.

WOW! Look at All this STUFF!

FiNALLY!!!!

I can kick off these high heels...
ZiNG
ZONG

... dump this "old Lady" disguise...

FWOOSH

...And start dressin' like my **True Self!**
RUB
RUB

A filthy...

...Rotten...

...Low-down...

FOOP!
...Good-for-nothin'...

... Deplorable...

... Contemptible...

...despicable...

... Loathsome...

...detestable...

...

Thesaurus

...Ignominious...

SUPERVILLAIN

And now, it's YOUR TURN!

Left hand here.

Right
Thumb
here.

Dude, we are **TOTALLY** Rockin' these bad guy costumes!

This is just for Pretend, though, right?

Sure, kid! It's **ALL** just make-believe!!!

CHAPTER 5

THE DOG-MAN
Sam E. Hamilton Presents
A GASSY Behemoth
Studios Production
THE DOG-Man
Starring Yolay Caprese · Scooter McRibs ·
Ding-Dong Magoo · And Samson J. Johnson as "Chief"
Soundtrack available on
GASSY Behemoth 8-tracks
DOGGY
K-9 Suitable For Canines
Some Material May be Too intense For Humans

POLICE
OLICE
ENOUGH IS ENOUGH!

I have HAD iT with these DOG-GONE Crimes in this DOG-Gone CiTY!!!
chief
crimes

Get me the DOG-MAN!!!
chief
Here I am, chief!

I'm Ready to ROLL!!!
chief

Whoops!
chief

CUT!
KLUNK
chief

BOSS
CHIEF

HEY!!!
BOSS

You're supposed to be guarding YOLAY CAPRESE!
BOSS

NOT Sleeping on the Set!

You made Ding-Dong Magoo trip and fall down!
YeAh!

You owe him an APOLOGY!!!
YEAH!

Lick
Lick
Lick

He Licked the inside of my mouth!!!
chief

I have HAD iT with these DOG-Gone DOG-Headed COPS in this DOG-Gone DOG-MAN Movie!
CHIEF

DOG MAN, YOU'RE FiRED!
COSA SUCCEDE?*
*What's Going on???

DOG Man has been MESSinG UP This Movie ALL DAY!

FirST, he wrecked the big ROMANCE SCENE!

DOG-Man, I think I'm falling in-
Sniff
Sniff

chomp!

CUT!

Then he ruined the big **Dramatic** Scene!

Don't You die on me!!! Don't You die on me!!!
chief

chief
P.U.!!! Who cut The cheese?

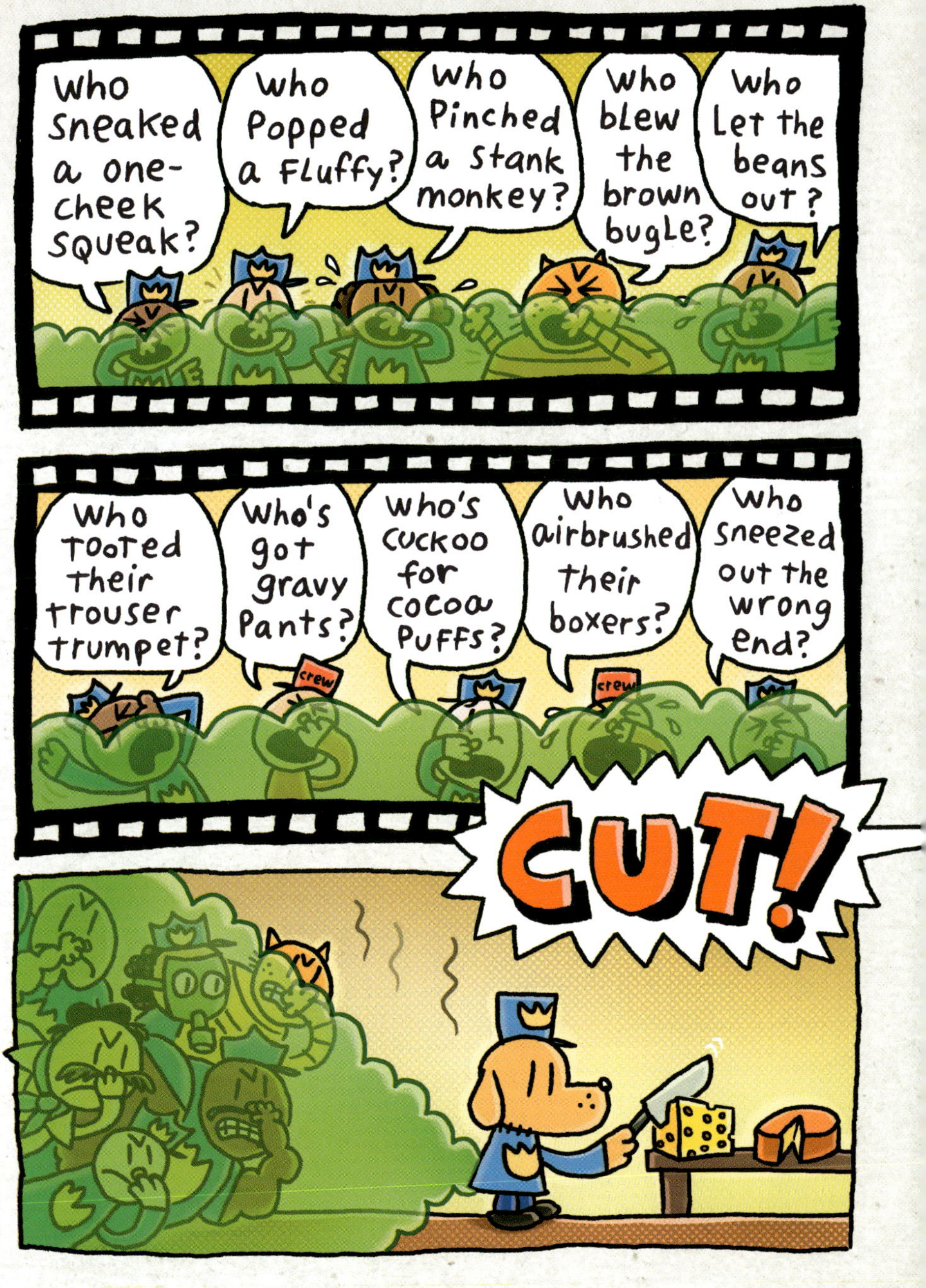

Who tooted their trouser trumpet?

Who's got gravy pants?

Who's cuckoo for cocoa puffs?

Who airbrushed their boxers?

Who sneezed out the wrong end?

crew

crew

CUT!

Left hand here.

Right
Thumb
here.

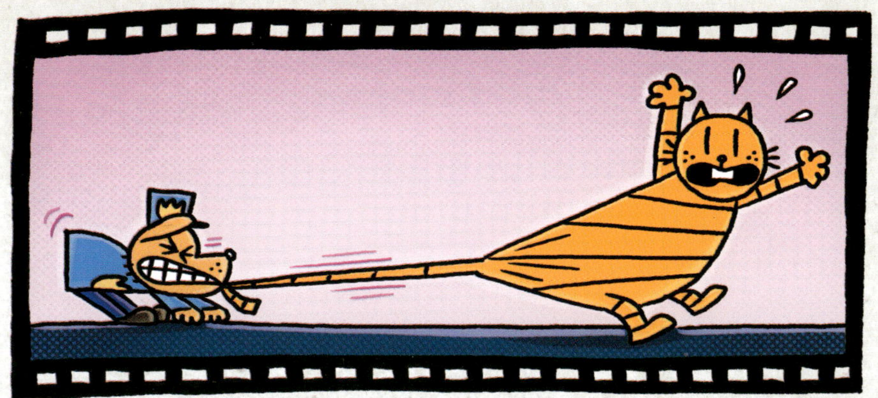

CUT!

You've been a BAD DOGGY!

GO HOME, DOG MAN!!

But Sam—
Sorry, Yolay. We've had Too many Problems...

...And if ONE MORE BAD Thing happens...

I'll have to Shut this WhOLE Movie Down!

Interesting!

Chapter 6

THE BARK KNIGHT RISES

COPS
COP

UH-Oh!
chief

He's gonna jump on me!
chief

He's gonna Lick my face!!!
chief

I can't take it!
chief

Spare me the indignity!!!
chief

chief

HEY!!!
chief

He's over here, Chief!
He's hiding behind that Plant again!
chief

What did you do THIS time?
Were you a bad doggy AGAIN?
chief

Leave him ALONE!
chief

Everybody makes mistakes!!!
chief

chief

COPS
chief

chief
I don't know what happened, Dog Man...

...but everything will be OK.
Chief

chief

Go home and get some rest!
chief

Tomorrow is another day!

DOG
Man

Lick
Lick

DOG
Man

Rub
RUB
Rub
RUB
Rub
FLIP FLOP

DOG MAN
FLip FLOP FLip

But Then...
SCReeeCH!

FLiP

K-SHONK!
80-HD
Primary Directives

80-HD
Primary Directive:
OBEY LI'L Petey

KA-TUNK!

Wait here for me, 80-HD!

80-HD
Primary Directive:
OBEY Li'L Petey

wait here for me, 80-HD!

Oh, hi Dog Man! How's it going?
RUFF!

Oh, NO!!! Is Li'l Petey missing again?

We just saw him! He was with his nanny!!!

What? What's wrong??? TELL ME!!!

OK. One word!

First syllable.

Do you have to pee???

Second syllable.

Are you drinking something?

Coffee?

tea?

Hmmm... The first syllable is "Pee."

And the second syllable is "tea."

Pee-tea?

Peetea?

PETEY?

Are you telling me that Petey disguised himself as a NANNY?

And that he was mistakenly hired to babysit Li'l Petey?

And at this very moment, he may be planning something EVIL?

And even while we speak, Li'l Petey may be drawn into this foulness...

LET'S GO SAVE THE WORLD!

GASSY BEHEMOTH STUDIOS
Guard
This is where we just saw them!

BUT...

BANNED
From the set
Do Not Let this cop inside!!!
Guard

OK, Dog Man...

...We're gonna go find Chief...

...You must find another way to get inside!!!

GASSY BEHEMOTH STUDIOS
Guard

GASSY
BEHEMOTH
STUDIOS

STUDIOS
Guard

STUDIOS
Guard
HEY!
POP

SO!!! You Thought you'd dig a Tunnel into the Studio, huh?
Guard

Looks like you popped up in the WRONG SPOT!

What an IDIOT!
Guard

You're coming with Me!!!
Guard
zip!

GASSY BEHEMOTH STUDIOS
HEY! COME BACK HERE!

GASSY BEHEMOTH STUDIOS
When I get my hands on YOU...

GASSY BEHEMOTH STUDIOS
...You're gonna wish you were NEVER Born!

GASSY BEHEMOTH STUDIOS
BANNED From The Lot
Do NOT LET This cop inside!!!
Guard
Come on and Show your face, ya filthy animal!!!

YA MANGY MUTT!
Guard

YA DUMB Jerk!!
Guard

YA dirty old Flea-bag!!!
Guard

YA glorified crossing guard!
Guard

YA Cheese-Faced WATer buFFaLo!
Guard

Ya GooFy-eyed Snickerdoodle!
Guard

WHOA!

KLUNK

STUDI
BANNED From The LoT
DO NOT LET This cop inside!!!
HEY!!!

Cameras
Make-up

If I see that Little Dog-headed cop again...
crew

There's gonna be **BIG TROUBLE!**
crew

Costumes

Chapter 7
A Buncha Stuff That Happened Next

I've Finally figured out a plan to Shut this movie DOWN!!!

C'mon, Kid!

Don't call me "kid." Call me "Cat Kid."

Why?
It's my Superhero name!

We're NOT Super HeroES!!! We're Super VILLAINS!

We're the BAD GUYS, Remember?
Oh, yeah!

The Pretend bad guys.

Right?

C'mon Cat KiD!!!
YAY!

So we can capture YoLay Caprese in this Lasso!!!

Why?

If they don't have a star, they can't finish the movie!

Why?

Meanwhile...

OK, People! We're about to Shoot the big action scene!

Are the mini-motor scooters in place?
Yes, sir!
crew

Is the Dogmobile gassed up?
Yep-er!
crew

Are the robotic hot dogs ready?
Ummmm...
EDEN

I lost the controller.
YOU WhaT?
EDEN

I just set it down at lunchtime, and now it's **Gone**!!!
EDEN

You've lost the controller!!!!
EDEN

How could things get any **worse**?
EDEN

VROOOOOOM!
EDEN

Skeeeeeeeeee
EDEN

ZOOOOOOOM!
EDEN

ZZZ
EDEN

ZiP
EDEN

GASSY BEHEMOTH STUDiOS
CRASH!
BANNED FROM THE SET
DO NOT LET THIS COP INSIDE!!!
?

How to operate the Dog-Mobile
How to operate the Dog-Mobile

mash
mash
PULL PULL
PULL

Screeech!

THONK

CHUNKA
CHUNKA

choppa
choppa
choppa
choppa

choppa
choppa
choppa
choppa
oppa

choppa
choppa
chop

GASSY BEHEMOTH STUDIOS
BANNED From The LoT
Do NOT LeT This cop inside!!!
Guard
Grunt
Grunt
Grunt

Well, it Took forever...
Guard

...but I finally got out of that hole!
Guard

And I vow here and now...
Guard

...To get my sweet revenge against That crazy Dog-headed cop!

Guard

GASSY
BEHEMOTH
ZOOOM
DO NOT LET This cop inside!!!

KLUNK

HEY!!

Meanwhile...
The Robot controller is Lost...

...the Dog-Mobile is missing...

...and there's a hole in the side of my studio!

How Could Things Get Any Worse?
Oh, Sam...

HEY!!!
ZIP
YOLAY!
COSA* SUCCEDE?
*What's going on?

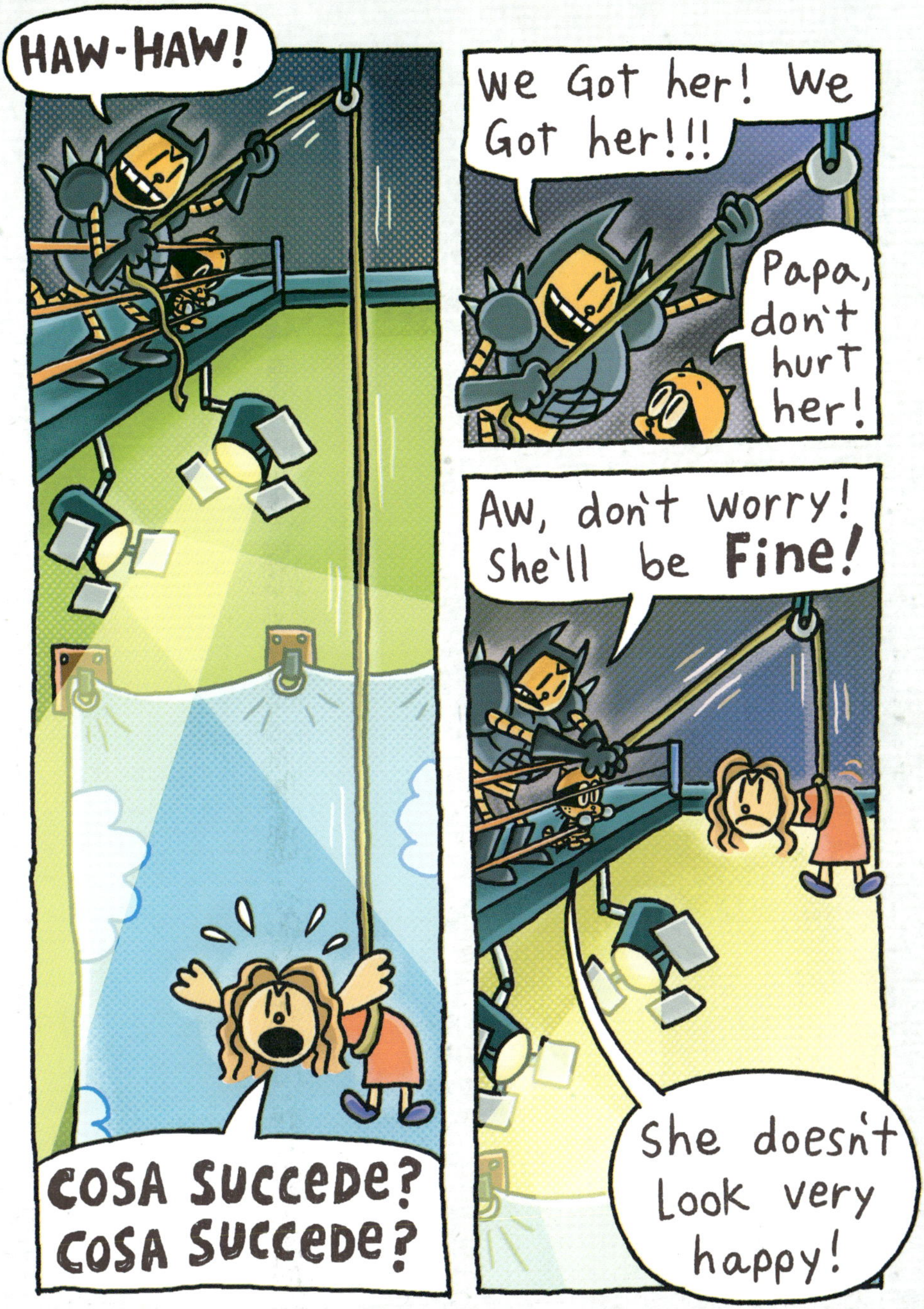

HAW-HAW!

COSA SUCCEDE?
COSA SUCCEDE?

Let's put her back, ok?

NO! We're the BAD GUYS!!!

WE DO EVIL STUFF!
But Papa-

Look, the world is NOT A very Nice Place!!!

It's Rotten---
It's UNFAIR---
It's HORRIBLE!

And the only way to get ahead...

...is to be even
More Rotten...
SAMUEL HAMILTON'S
GASSY
BEHEMOTH
STUDIOS

...MORE
UNFAIR...

...AND MORE
HORRIBLE!
THOUG

Check out our brand-new motto!!!
THOUGHTLESS MAYHEM IS BEST

NOW--- Do ya wanna have some REAL FUN???

Cut her down!

Use those steel claws of yours and slice the rope!

NO, PAPA!
AW COME ON!!!

Don't be a baby!!! Cut that Rope!!!
NO!

THOU SHALT OBEY!!!

THOU SHALT FOLLOW THY DESTINY!!!

THOU SHALT!

THOU SHALT!

THOU SHALT!

G
THO
M
T
I
M

CRASH
AY
EST
E
SHEL
B

THOU
MAYEST

MAYEST
Thou mayest.

THOU SHALT!
Thou mayest!

THOU SHALT
Thou mayest!
THOU SHALT
Thou mayest! Thou mayest! Thou mayest!

THOU
MAYEST!!!

PBBBT

SHiNG
SHiNG

SHHHHHH

SHHH

SHOOF
PAINT
PAINT
TWANG
PAINT

HELMETS

zeeez

SLICE

GASSY
BEHEMOTH
STUDIOS
CRASH

SKRRRR

ZZEEEEEEEE

EXIT
EXIT
ZMMMM

GASSY BEHEMOTH STUDIOS
BANNED From The Lot
Do NOT LeT This cop inside!!!
GUARD
Grunt
Grunt

GASSY BEHEMOTH STUDIOS
BANNED From The Lot
BAM

BANNED From The Lot
Do NOT LeT This cop inside!!!
HEY!

Bubbida-bubbida-b

bubbida-bubbida-bubbid

bubbida- bubbida-bubbida
FOOOOOOOSH

ZAP
SWOOOOOOOSH
CIRCUS
Wow!
Sweeet!
Cool, Right?

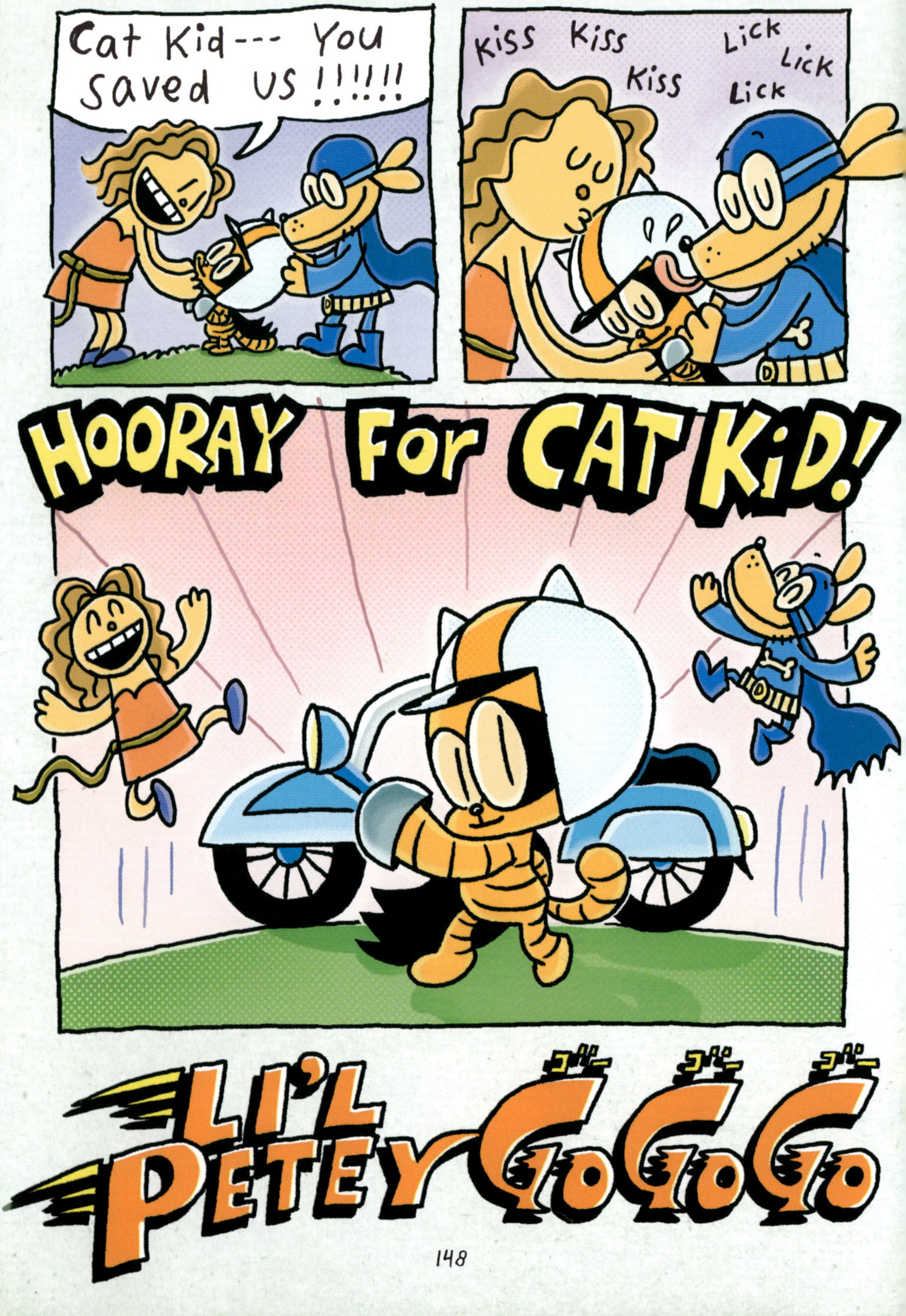

HOORAY For CAT KiD!

CHAPTER 8
DESTROY ALL WEENIES

Meanwhile...
STUDIOS
GASSY BEHEMOTH STUDIOS
BANNED From the Lot
Do not let this cop inside!!!
Grunt
Grunt
Grunt

I have **HAD it** with these **Dog-Gone Disasters** in this **DOG-Gone STUDIO!!!**
chief

I QUIT!
Me Too!
Me Three!
But Fellas---
chief

GASSY BEHEMOTH STUDIOS
BANNED
From
SET
BONK

I'm Ruined!

How Could Things get Any worse?

ON OFF
GOOD E
ON OFF
GOOD EViL
ON OFF
GOOD EViL
ZAP

ZAP
EDEN
EDEN MECHA-BOTS
EN
EDEN

GRRRRR
Eden
EDEN MECHA-BOTS
Eden
Eden

ATTACK!

Grunt
Grunt
Grunt
CRASH!

I'm gonna Get That dog-headed cop...
GUArd

...if it's the **Last thing I...**
Guard

CRASH
GUArd

...DOOOOOOOooooo...

KLUNK

Soon, the Mecha-weenies began to Organize!

Listen up, bubs! We gotta DESTROY THIS CITY!

Oh, Look at the little cutie pies!!!

Left hand here.

Right Thumb here.

BASTA!!*
(*Enough!!)

I Think we're gonna have to fight these guys!

But you can't eat 'em, DOG Man!!!

They're **ROBOTS!**

That's **RIGHT!** And you guys are **OUTNUMBERED** thirty to **Three!**

Correction: Thirty to SIX!!!
chief

Who Are You Guys?

I'm Purse LADY!
Bearer of the Purse!

This is SUPA-FANG!
Grrrrrr!

And I'm Chief!
chief

Psst--- Don't say your real name!
chief

Make up a Superhero name!
Oh, yeah!

chief
Hmmm...

I'm **CHIEF MAN!**
chief

HAW HAW
HAW HAW
What?

You guys are the DUMbest Super-heroes I've ever Seen!

Purse LAdy?

What's So Scary about a PUrse???

HAW
HAW

BAM

You're GONNA-
POW
I'm GONNA-
WHACK
TRIPLE FLIP-O-RAMA
Left hand here.

Right Thumb here.

And So...

Are you OK, boss?

DUHR--- Me Go Baby Poo-Poo Pee-Pee!

So...

...Does anybody ELSE think I'm a dumb Superhero?

YAAAAAAA!

chief
Bye-bye, nice Lady!

RATS!

I Can't BeLieve it!!!

PUNX

Those IDiOT Mecha-Weenies just GAVE UP!

But I'm NOT Giving up!

I've got ONE FiNAL PLAN!

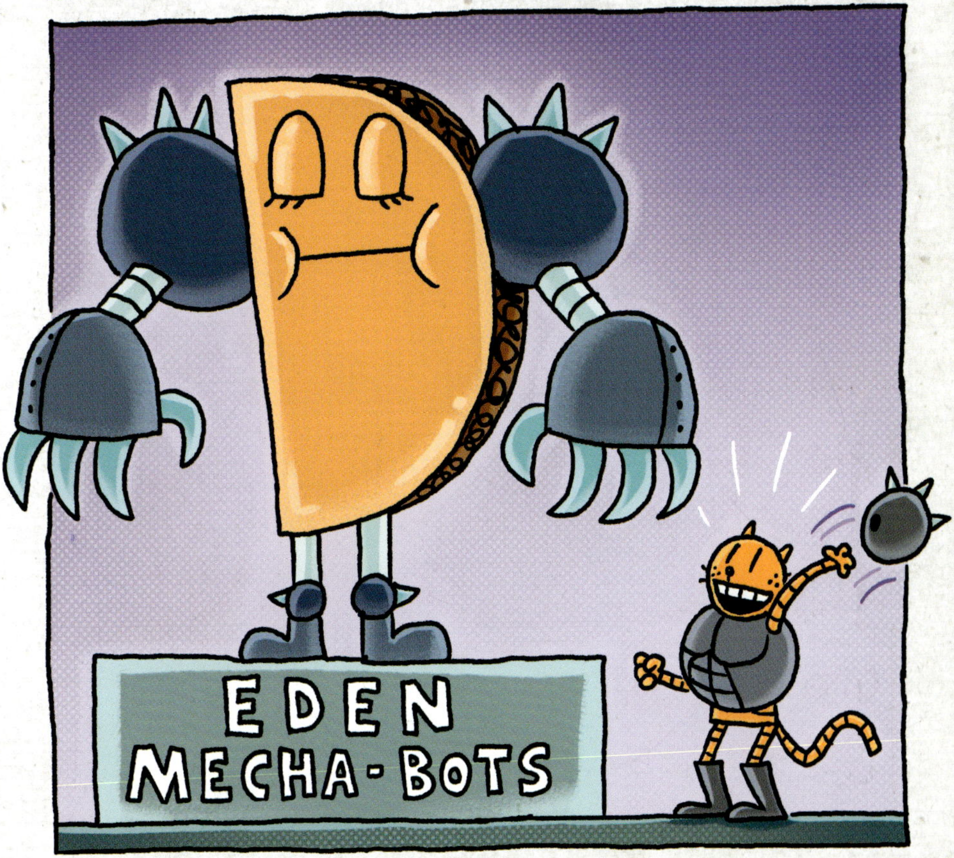

EDEN MECHA-BOTS

If only I could make him bigger!

I need a super Growth formula!

Something Convenient!

Preferably in a non-aerosol spray!!!

Hey! Wait a minute...

BONK

...I know just where to go!!!
IOTH
IOS

Chapter 9
CANNERY GROW
MAGIC GROWTH FORMULA
Makes Anything Grow!

Quick! I Need A CAN OF CANNERY Grow!

Hi. Welcome to Cannery GLOW!

HI! I NEED A CAN OF CANNERY GROW!!!

How may I help you?

I NEED A CAN OF CANNERY Grow!

WeLL Why didn't you say so in the First PLace?

Can I have your Phone number?

WHY??? WHAT For???

It's for our computer.

ONE-TWO-Three-four-Five-Six-SeVEN-Eight-Nine-TEN!!!

OK, Let's see here...

Hmmmmm...

Uhhh...

Dum-dee-dum-
dee-dum...

One!
click

Hmmmm...

Ummmm...

Lemme think
now...

What comes After ONE???

Wait--- Don't tell me---

WOULD YOU HURRY it UP?

YA just made me Lose count!

Now I have to start all over!!!

Uhhh...

TWENTY-TWO MINUTES LATER...

Ten!
CLICK

NOW can I buy a can of Cannery Grow?
WELL...

...Do you have a Cannery Grow frequent buyer's card?

NO!
Would you like to apply for one?
NO!

I DON'T WANT A CANNERY GROW FREQUENT BUYER'S CARD!

ALRIGHT, ALRIGHT!

YOU'RE NOT A VERY NICE PERSON!

I WAS JUST doin' my JOB!

ALL I wanted to do was Help you!!!

I tried my best, but...

...Ya didn't have to be so MEAN!

ALL ya had to DO WAS ASK NiCELY!!!!

I have FeeLings ya KNOW!!!

I'm sorry. You're right!
HONK RAGS

I'LL ask niceLy, ok?
HONK!

May I PLease have a can of cannery Grow?

Sorry, we're closed Today!
ZONG!

I'm TAKinG This!!!

Oh yeah? Well I'm Callin' 9-1-1 !!!

Let's see now... uh...

CANNERY GROW
Ummm...
MAGiC GROWTh FORMULA
MAKES AnyThing Grow!

And so...

EDEN MECHA-BOTS

shake

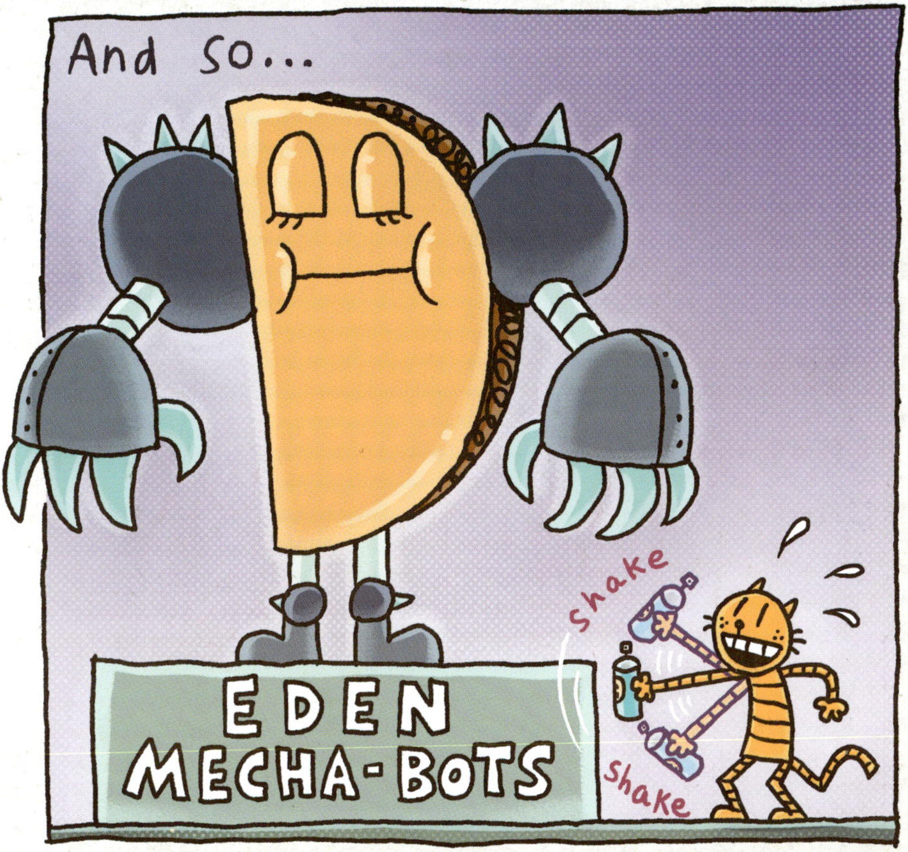

shake

SQUIRT
SQUIRT
SQUIRT
EDEN
MECHA-BOTS

EDEN
MECHA-BOTS

EDEN
MECHA-BOTS

CHAPTER 10

BEAST OF EDEN

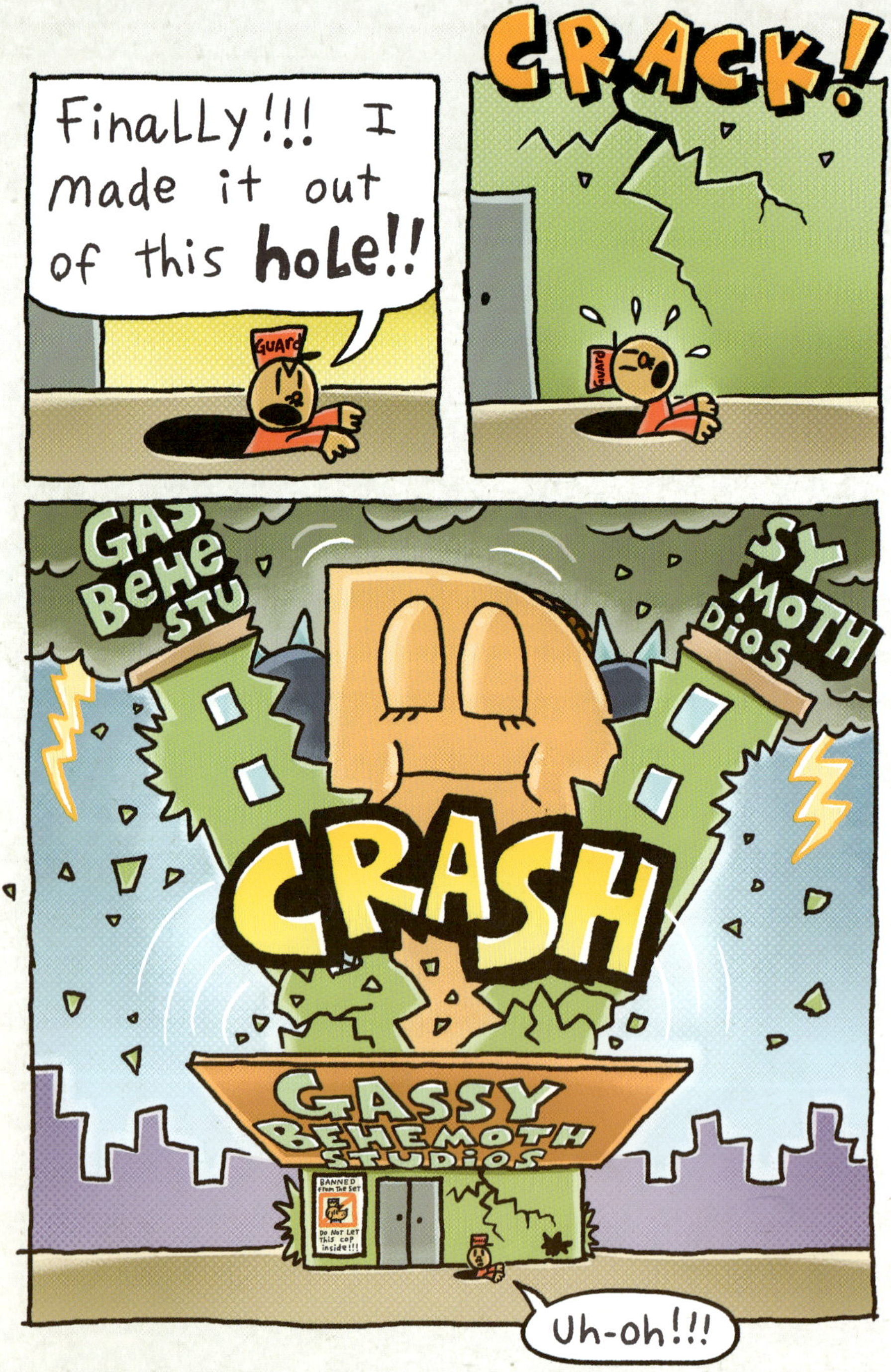

GAS BeHe STU

SY MOTH DiOS

CRASH

GASSY BEHEMOTH STUDIOS

BANNED from the set

Do Not Let This cop inside!!!

Uh-oh!!!

BANNED From the set
Do not let this cop inside!!!
FOOMP!
HEY!
And Now, for the FINAL TOUCH!
ZAP
ON OFF
GOOD EVIL

Uh-Oh!
Here comes Trouble!!!
chief

chief
SWOOSH

chief
chief
chief

ZOOM

SHING
SHING
SLICE

HAW-HAW!!!!!
YA **Missed!**

TRIPLE FLIP-O-RAMA

Left hand here.

Right Thumb here.

CHIEF

Hang on, Lady!

I'LL get help!!!

SKEEEEEE
ZMMM
HEY!!!
CAT KID!! COME BACK!

ZMMMMMM

Hi, 80-HD!
DOG MAN

You gotta come with me! We need your help!

FLip FLOP FLip FLop FLip FLOP

He's Just OBeying you!

I Programmed him to do that!!!

He's Not **REALLY** your friend!!!

OBedience And Friendship Are **NOT** the Same things!!!

Objects in mirror may NOT be as close as They appear.

FLIP FLOP FLIP FLO
SCREETCH
Open up, 80-HD!

Enter main Programming mode.

K-SHONK

80-HD
Primary Directive:
OBey Li'L Petey

Shing Shing

Delete
Delete
Delete
Delete
Delete
Delete
Delete
80-HD
Primary Directive:
OBey L_

80-HD
Primary Directive:
scratch
scratch

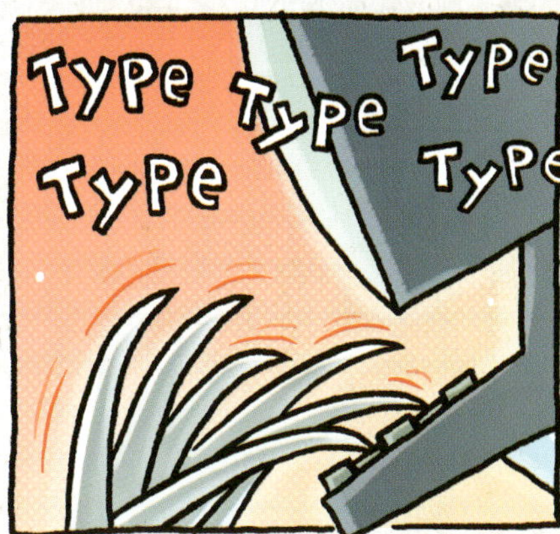
Type
Type
Type
Type
Type

These are important words, 80-HD.

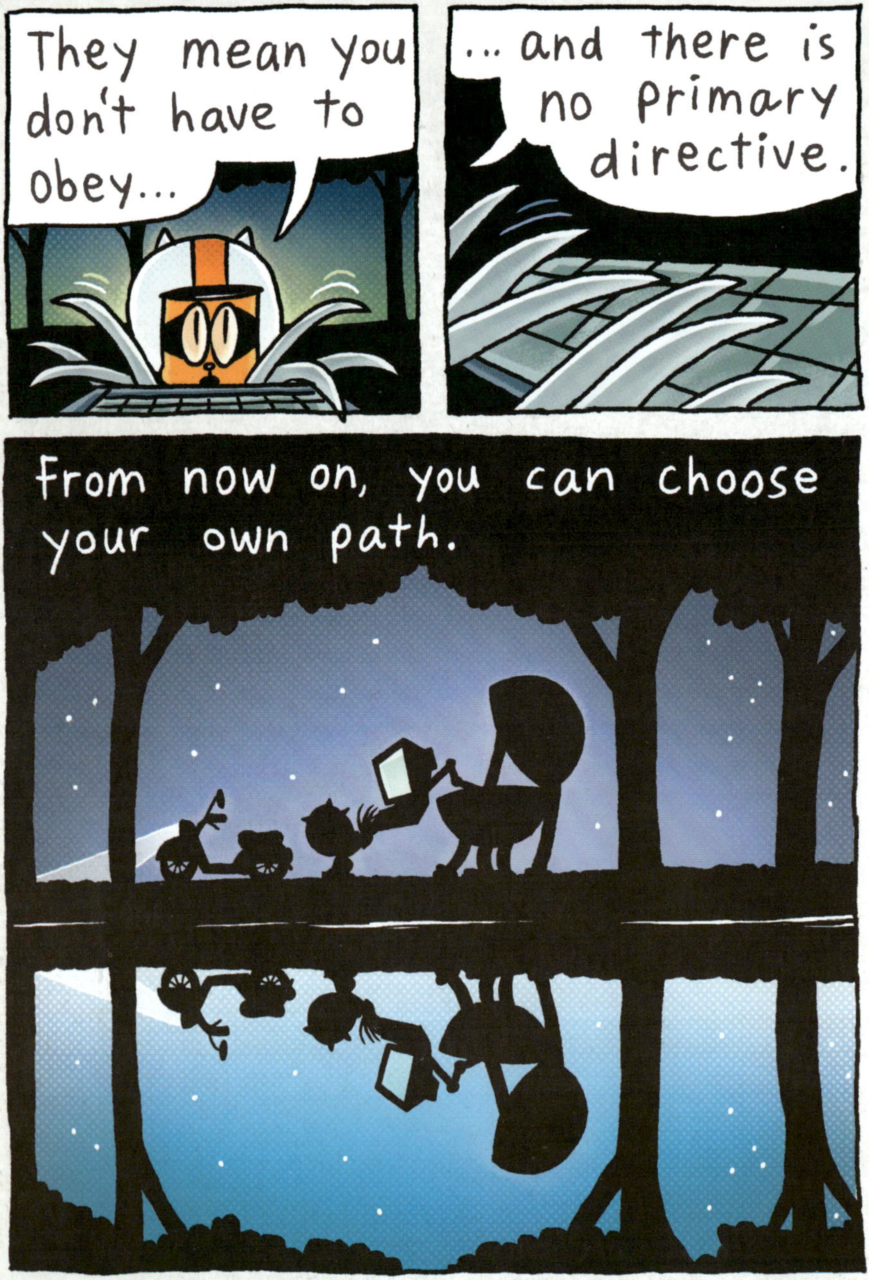

From now on, you can choose your own path.

80-HD
Thou mayest

Reboot

CLICK
Rebo

80-HD
Thou mayest

CHUNKA-CHUNKA

You don't have to be my friend anymore.

You don't have to-

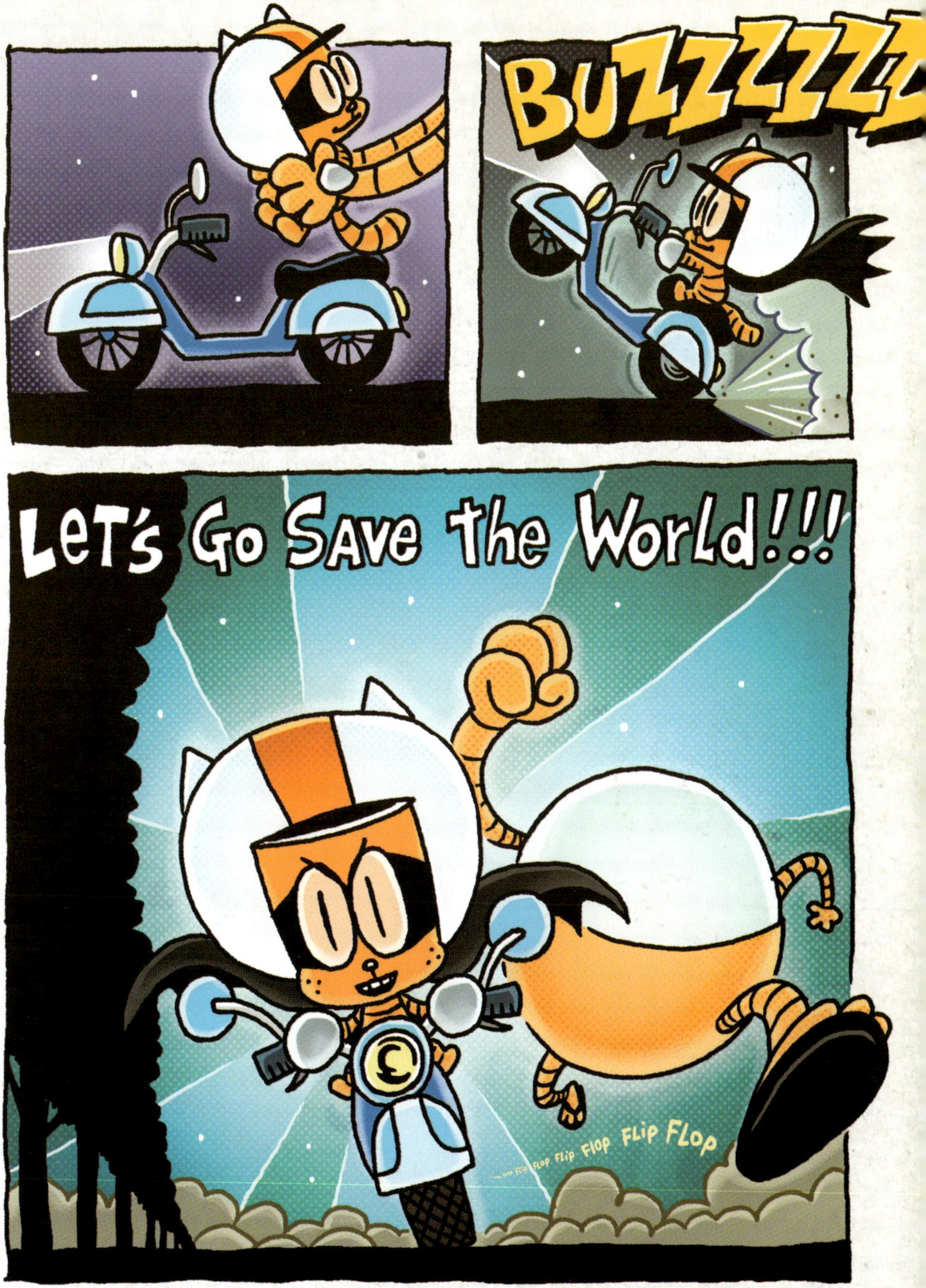

LET'S Go Save the World!!!

Flip Flop Flip Flop Flip Flop

Soon...
WELL, WELL, WELL... Look who's BACK!!!
Zeeeee

I captured all of your friends while you were gone!
chief

Not all of them!

Get ready to get your butt kicked...

...by my good friend 80-HD!!!

Hey 80-HD!!! Where'd ya go?

This I Gotta see!

80-HD!!!

The "AMAZING" Cat Kid replaced all of 80-HD's Atomic batteries with...

...SOLAR PANELS!

It's been cloudy ALL DAY LONG—
So 80-HD couldn't charge up!!!

And Now it's Night-Time!
Power Level: 0.0%

What's the matter, 80-HD?
Are ya feelin' a Little Run-down?

Maybe he just needs a little **KICK**!!!

PAPA! NO!!!

NOOOOO!!!
WHAM!

Yep! I was RiGht!!!

All he needed was a little kick!!!
Pat Pat
WAAAAAA

Aw, Quit your Belly-AcHiN'!!!

He WAS ONLY A RoboT...

Stop being such a baby!!!

He WASN'T even your Friend!!!

And besides---
friends don't matter anyway!

It's All About FAMiLY!!!

Your BLOOD!
Your ROOTS!
Your DESTINY!

THAT'S what's important!

ONE HOUR LATER...

IF you don't Stop Crying, I'm gonna---

I'm gonna---

I'm gonna---

SLice
CHIEF
SPLASH

We're Free!!!
CRASH!

Chief
US Too!
SMASH!

WHAT HAPPened? WAS it A MeteoR???

...A Comet???
...An Asteroid???

80-HD!???!

How'd ya do it? How'd ya get your power back???
Chief

Art Supplies

Draw Draw Draw

fold fold fold

staple staple staple

Chapter 11

Of Rice and Yen

A mini-Comic
by 80-HD

おにぎり 100円
おにぎり 100円
Power Level: 39%

Power Level: 78.0%
Power Level: 100%

おにぎり 100円
おにぎり 100円

おにぎり
100円

Chapter 12
TimsheL
DOG
Man

HOORAY For 80-HD!!!
Phooey!

Well, Petey, it's Time to take you to Cat Jail!!!
RATS!

You have the right to remain fluffy...
Hey, Kid...
click

...Anything you purr may be used against you...
Do ya wanna have Lunch together after I escape tomorrow?
OK!

...You have the right to a mouse-Shaped toy with a jingle bell inside...
CHIEF

IL Mio Eroe!*
* My Hero!!!

You were very brave today, bello mio!

Yeah...

...but I wasn't perfect.

I harbored a Fugitive...

...I Littered...
...I jaywalked...

...I even StoLe this CoStume.

I guess I'll never be perfect!

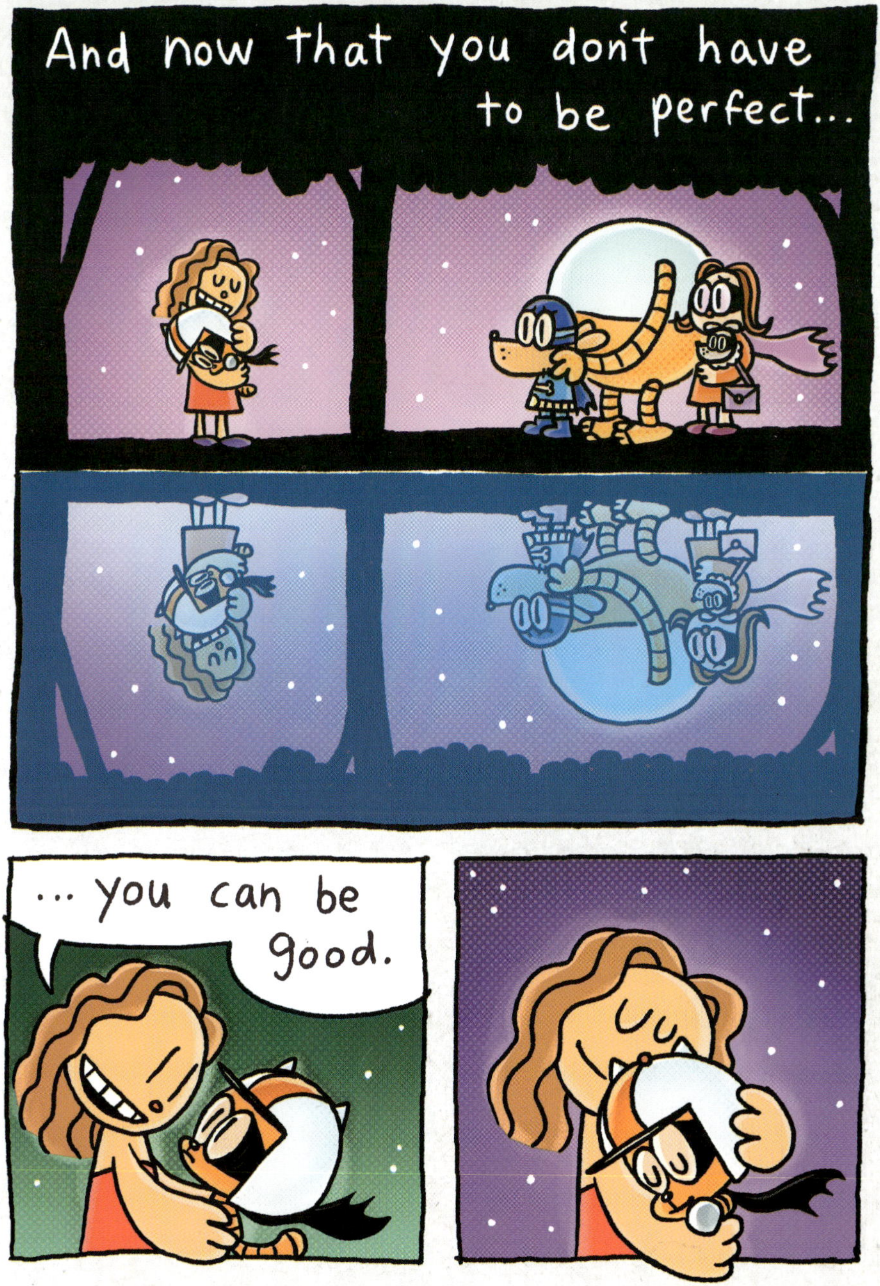

And now that you don't have to be perfect...

Well, good night!
Ciao! Buonanotte!
Let's play again Tomorrow!
FLIP FLOP FLIP

Oh, Look--- it's that guy!!!
FLIP FLOP FLIP

Hey Mister, we took some stuff from your movie studio.
So?

We wanna give it all back!
I don't care about that stuff!

I gotta scram before somebody makes me clean up this **MESS!**

And so...

I hope all this stuff fits inside our house.

DOG man

Flip Flop Flip Flop Flip Flop Flip

Yep. It does!

Flip Flop Flip Flop Flip

Now if we just had a special place where we could work together!

Can I press the button?

HEY!!!
Grand Ballroom

I didn't know our house had a grand ballroom!
Grand Ballroom
CLICK

DING

GRAND BALLROOM
Wow! It's a room full of balls!
FLIP FLOP FLIP
This is Grand!
PAT PAT
And so, the three friends worked and played together...
FLOP FLIP FLOP FLIP

... until it was time for bed.

DOG
Man

The End

BUT WAIT...

...if you thought our adventure was over...

YOU AIN'T READ NOTHIN' YET!

At this very moment, George and Harold are reading Another old-timey book...
Lord of the Flies William Golding
Lord of the Flies William Golding

... and getting a buncha New-Timey ideas!

So get ready for an epic tale...

...of depth, maturity, and intelligence.
sniff
sniff

Because a Brand-New Dog Man adventure is comin' your way!!!
FLIP FLOP FLIP FLOP FLIP

DOG MAN
LORD OF THE FLEAS
If You Like THRILLS...
...And you Like LAFFS...
...Then DOG MAN is GO!
DOG Man is Go?
That don't make no sense!!!
Whoops!
But we Like it!!!

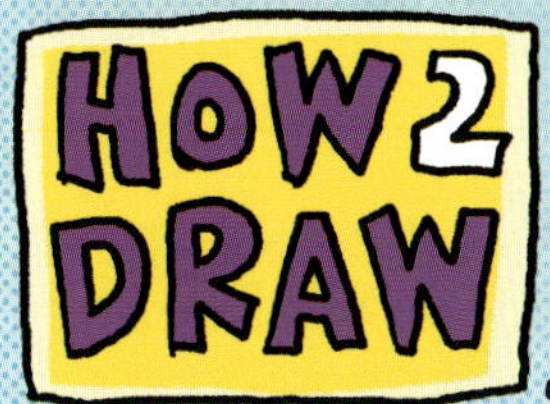

HOW 2 DRAW THE BARK KNIGHT

in 46 Ridiculously easy steps!

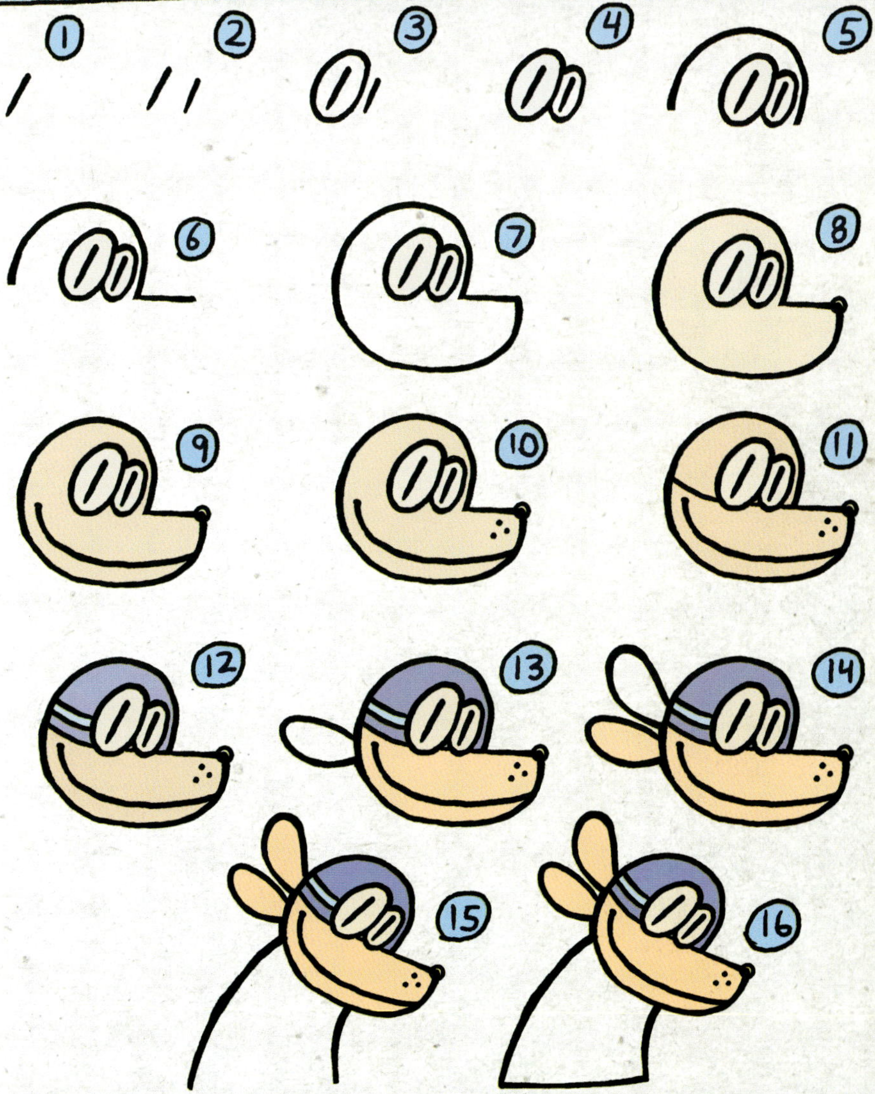
1
2
3
4
5
6
7
8
9
10
11
12
13
14
15
16

17
18
19
20
21
22
23
24
25
26
27
28
29
30
31
32
33
34

35
36
37
38
39
40
41
42
43
44
45
46

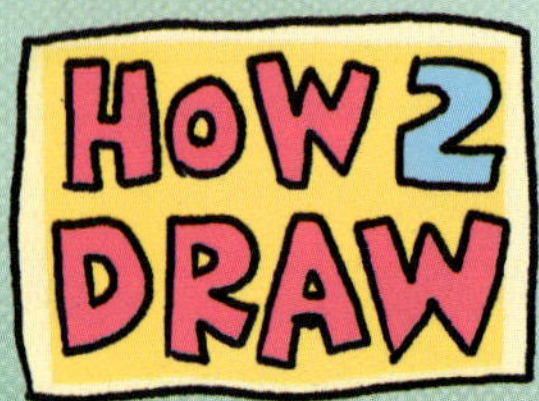

HOW 2 DRAW SUPA-MECHA PHILLY

in 37 Ridiculously easy steps!

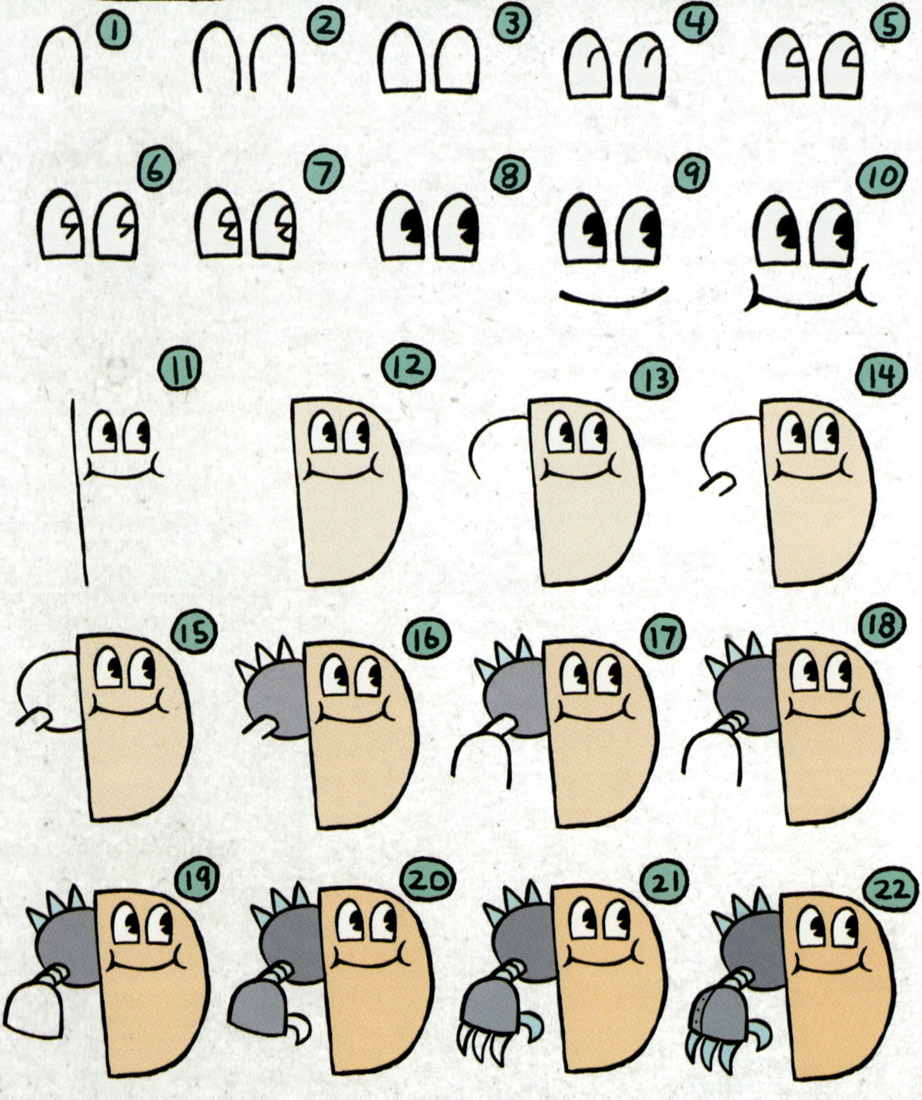
1
2
3
4
5
6
7
8
9
10
11
12
13
14
15
16
17
18
19
20
21
22

23
24
25
26
27
28
29
30
31
32
33
34
35
36
37

CAT KiD

in 39 Ridiculously easy steps!

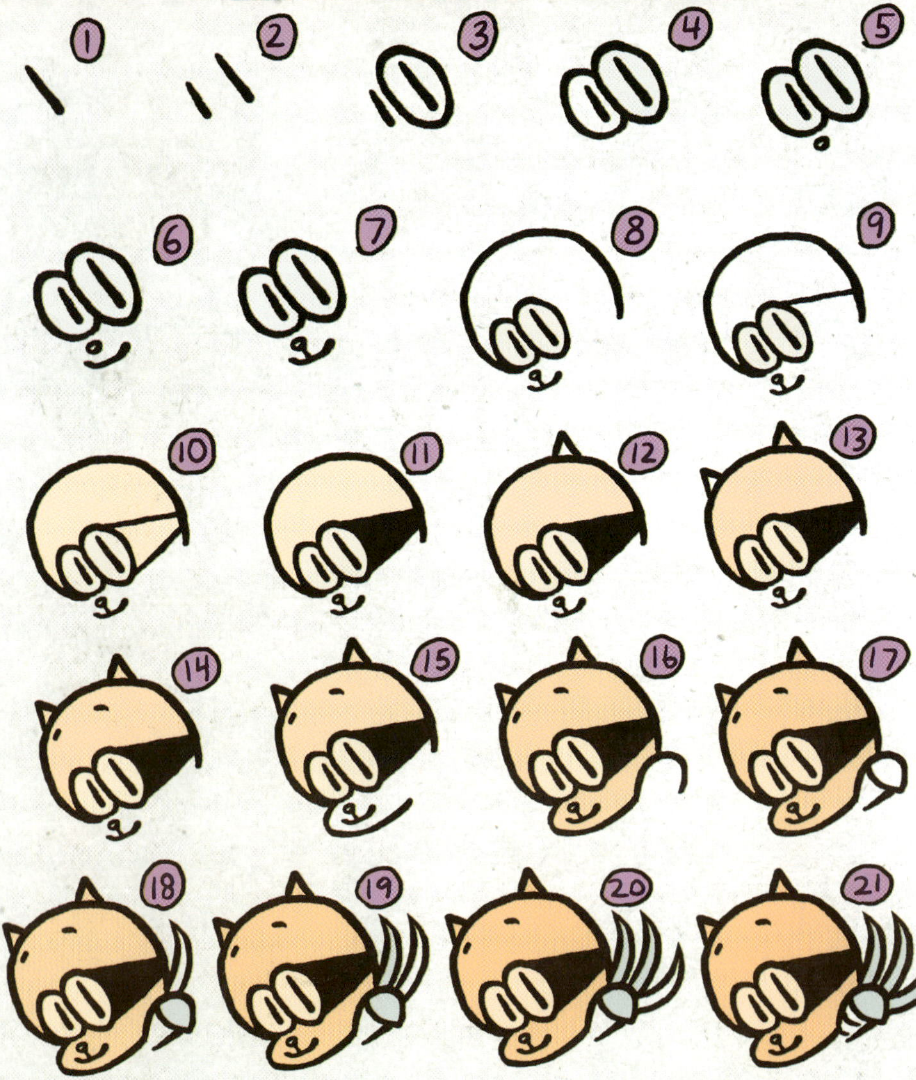

1 2 3 4 5

6 7 8 9

10 11 12 13

14 15 16 17

18 19 20 21

22
23
24
25
26
27
28
29
30
31
32
33
34
35
36

37
38
39

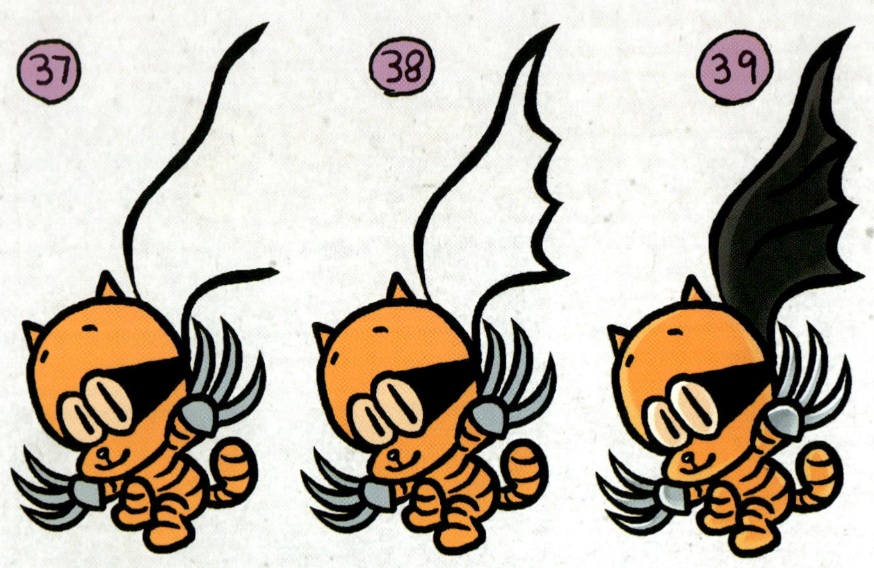

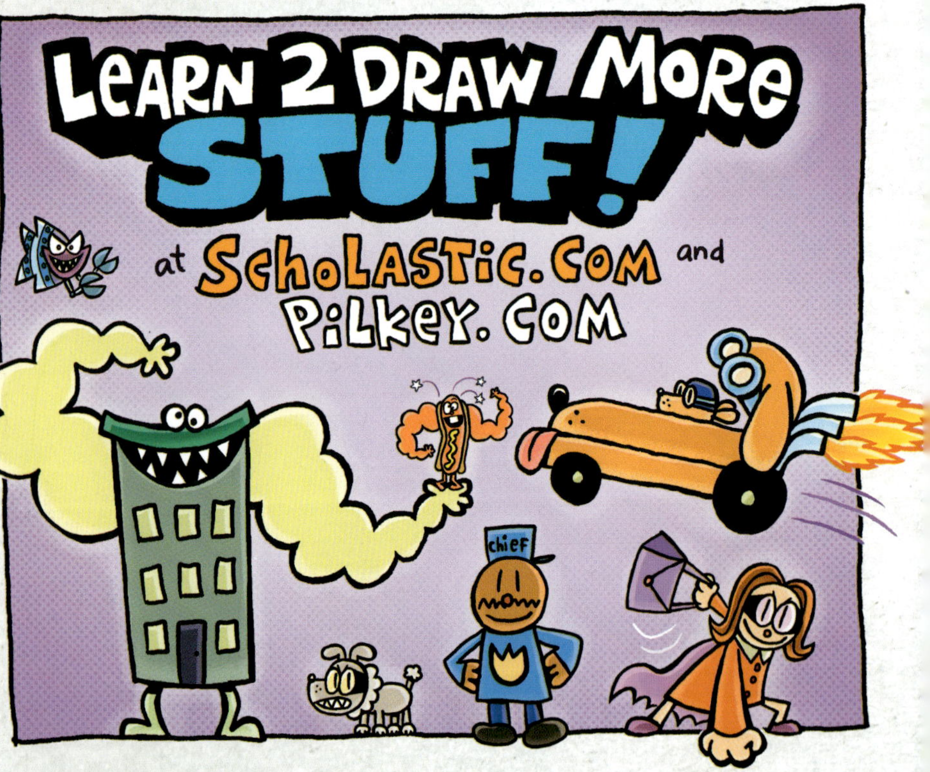
LEARN 2 DRAW MORE
STUFF!
at SCHOLASTIC.COM and
PILKEY.COM
chief

NOTES

by George and Harold

- ☆ The titles of chapters 9, 10, and 11 are parodies of the titles of <u>Other</u> books by John Steinbeck.

- ☆ The words on pages 57 and 233 are direct Quotes From <u>East of Eden</u> by Steinbeck.

- ☆ The Japanese words in chapter 11 mean: Onigiri (rice balls), 100 yen (about a dollar).

- ☆ "Timshel" is the Hebrew word For "Thou mayest."

GET READING WITH RICKY RICOTTA!

"A fun introduction to chapter books." — School Library Journal

"Has all the classic Pilkey hallmarks: comic book panels, superhero action, and Flip-O-Rama." — Booklist

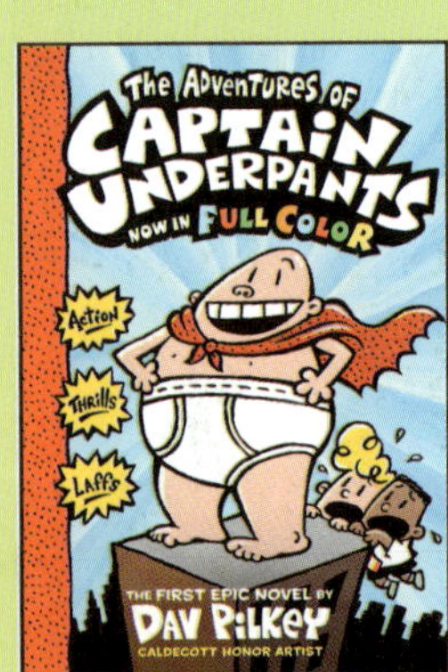

THE CRITICS ARE CRAZY ABOUT UNDERPANTS!

"Pilkey's sharp humor shines, and is as much fun for parents as their young readers." — Parents' Choice Foundation

"So appealing that youngsters won't notice that their vocabulary is stretching." — School Library Journal

KIDS ARE GAGA FOR GRAPHIC NOVELS!

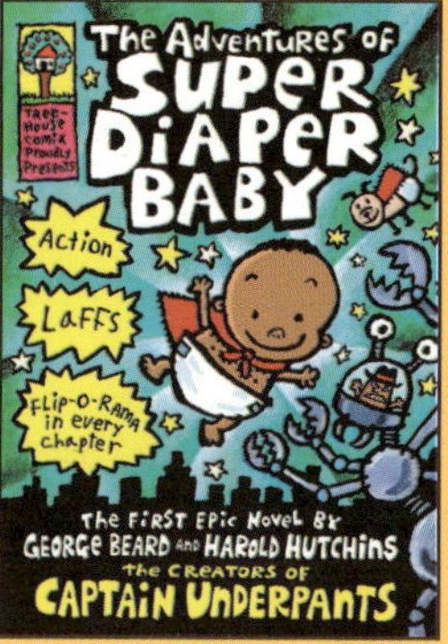

"The laughs here (and there are many) are definitely spot-on for the intended audience."
— School Library Journal

"Will appeal to those who like silly adventures."
— Booklist

FANS ARE DIGGING THE TOP DOG!

★"Riotously funny and original."
— School Library Journal, starred review

★"An utter, unfettered delight."
— Booklist, starred review

★"Readers (of any age) will be giggling from start to finish."
— Publishers Weekly, starred review

Download the free Planet Pilkey app to start your digital adventure! Create an avatar, make your own comics, and more at planetpilkey.com!

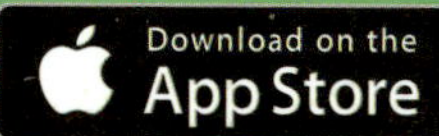

ABOUT THE AUTHOR-ILLUSTRATOR

When Dav Pilkey was a kid, he suffered from ADHD, dyslexia, and behavioral problems. Dav was so disruptive in class that his teachers made him sit out in the hall every day. Luckily, Dav loved to draw and make up stories. He spent his time in the hallway creating his own original comic books.

In the second grade, Dav Pilkey created a comic book about a superhero named Captain Underpants. His teacher ripped it up and told him he couldn't spend the rest of his life making silly books.

Fortunately, Dav was not a very good listener.

ABOUT THE COLORIST

Jose Garibaldi grew up on the South Side of Chicago. As a kid, he was a daydreamer and a doodler, and now it's his full-time job to do both. Jose is a professional illustrator, painter, and cartoonist who has created work for Dark Horse Comics, Disney, Nickelodeon, MAD Magazine, and many more. He lives in Los Angeles, California, with his wife and their cats.